TRUCKS

by Cheryl Klein & Katy Beebe

illustrated by Mike Boldt

Disney • HYPERION

LOS ANGELES   NEW YORK

Text copyright © 2019 by Cheryl Klein and Katy Beebe

Illustrations copyright © 2019 by Mike Boldt

Back Matter Sources:
National Severe Storms Laboratory. "Thunderstorm Basics." Severe Weather 101. Accessed
September 4, 2018. https://www.nssl.noaa.gov/education/svrwx101/thunderstorms/

National Severe Storms Laboratory. "Lightning Basics." Severe Weather 101. Accessed
September 4, 2018. https://www.nssl.noaa.gov/education/svrwx101/lightning/

The authors thank Dr. Kent McGregor of the University of North Texas for his expertise and advice.

First Edition, September 2019
10 9 8 7 6 5 4 3 2 1
FAC-029191-19207
Printed in Malaysia

This book is set in Otari/Fontspring and Neutratext/House Industries
Designed by Joann Hill and David Hastings

Library of Congress Cataloging-in-Publication Data
Names: Klein, Cheryl B., 1978- author. • Beebe, Katy, author. • Boldt, Mike, illustrator.
Title: Thunder Trucks / by Cheryl Klein and Katy Beebe ; illustrated by Mike Boldt.
Description: First edition. • Los Angeles : Disney Hyperion, 2019. • Summary:
As children go to sleep, trucks of all kinds team up in the sky to create a thunderstorm.
Identifiers: LCCN 2018053223• ISBN 9781368024600 (hardcover) • ISBN 1368024602 (hardcover)
Subjects: • CYAC: Stories in rhyme. • Thunderstorms—Fiction. •
Trucks—Fiction. • Bedtime—Fiction.
Classification: LCC PZ8.3.K6573 Th 2019 • DDC [E]—dc23
LC record available at https://lccn.loc.gov/2018053223

Reinforced binding

Visit www.DisneyBooks.com

For Melissa, Joe, Callum, and
Poppy Jackson, with love
—C.B.K.

For the Primos—Nathan, Eden,
Asher, Isaac, and José
—K.B.

For Eli
—M.B.

Whisper, roll, rattle. Grumble, bump, beep.
Just when you're settling down to sleep,

you might hear a rumbling,
tumbling sound.
That means the Thunder Trucks
are gathering 'round!

Bulldozer growls as she shoves through the sky, pushing puffs into thunderheads three miles high.

When Crane Truck helps
with his powerful boom,
the clouds stack tall
and the wind goes

ZOOM!

Thunder Trucks loud. Thunder Trucks strong.
Thunder Trucks moving this storm along.

We've got a good team in Dozer and Crane.
Now Tanker Truck's here to bring the rain!

With a grind of his brakes, he greets the band,
but the rain's in his tank, and he needs a hand.

Fire Truck races through the fray,
loaded with hoses that bubble and spray.

He heaves out a line and starts his pump,
and soon those raindrops spatter and jump.

Chug-chug,

honk-honk,

skitter-skatter,

SPLASH!

The next truck approaches with a clangorous crash.

In bustles Dump Truck, filled to the brink.

"Hail-o, friends,"
she says with a wink.

The crew toot their horns
as she joins the jam.

"*Pssssssshhh!*" Dump says
as she lifts her rams.

The rams tilt
the dumper bed
up, up, up,

and down pour
the hailstones—

thump,
thump,
thump!

Thunder Trucks loud.
Thunder Trucks strong.

Thunder Trucks moving this storm along.

Clouds and rain
and hail—all set.
But this big storm's
not over yet!

Fire Truck can do
way more than splash.
He lights his beacons,
and with a flash—

ZIP! runs the lightning in a glorious arc,
forking and fizzing and spitting out sparks!

The signal zaps out with a dazzling **CRACK** and in no time at all there's an answer back.

With a clamor and a racket and a rattling din,
the last of the crew comes barreling in.

Blowing her horn as she bursts through the gloom,
Big Rig's hauling THUNDER with a

BOOM
BOOM BOOM BOOM

The trucks rev their motors with a mighty roar.
This is the moment that they've waited for!

They divvy up the thunder and they roll out wide,
and the whole sky rumbles with power and pride.

THUNDER TRUCKS LOUD!
THUNDER TRUCKS STRONG!

THUNDER TRUCKS
THUNDERING
ALL NIGHT LONG!

Once the thunder is settled and gone,
the trucks circle back with a stretch and a yawn.

They push off the clouds and fold up Crane,
whip up some hail, and refill the rain.

"Good work," they call, and "See you soon!"
And away they coast 'neath a bright round moon:

Dozer and Crane in the sparkling sky,
Tanker, Fire, Dump, Big Rig . . .

Good-bye!

So if you hear thunder
    in the dark of night,
        don't fly undercover
            or flip on the light.

        Just wave overhead
            to your friends having fun. . . .

Good night, Thunder Trucks.

Job well done!

The Real Science Behind Storms

Heating Up: Storms actually begin with the sun, which heats the air. Because warm air is lighter than the cooler air around it, the warmer air rises into the sky.

Cooling Off: That warm air keeps moving upward until it begins to cool again. When it is cool enough, the moisture in the air condenses, creating the white clouds that we see.

Growing Tall: As these clouds are swept up by the warm air still rising around them, they grow taller and taller.

Falling Down: The taller and cooler the clouds grow, the more moisture condenses, forming raindrops. These raindrops are heavy, so they fall down to earth. This is when the fun really starts!

- Lighter raindrops can be blown upward to the cool air at the top of the cloud, where they freeze into hail and fall once more.
- When small drops of ice, water, and air rub against one another in the cloud, they build up an electric charge. When the balance of the charge tips one way or the other— *ZAP!*—we see arcs of electricity in the form of lightning.
- All that electricity heats the air around it to an incredible temperature—about 18,000 degrees Fahrenheit! This hot air builds up until it EXPLODES out of the cloud as thunder.

Drifting Away: Eventually, the energy of the storm begins to slow down. The clouds break up and the sky clears . . . until the next time!